A
Giving
Soul
Ellena Muhammad
rewards in keeping faith

Ordering Information:
You may search this book in Amazon, Barnes & Nobles and other online retailers by searching using the ISBN below.

ISBN (Hardcover): 978-1-956135-60-2

TABLE OF CONTENTS

Dedicated: To Good People

For: MALICHI

CHAPTER ONE

From a boy to a man

Once there was a boy named Jacob. Ever since Jacob was born, everyone noticed his unique personality. He was always a very giving person. Jacob once a young boy, grew into a stern man. Early in Jacob's life, his parents passed away to a mysterious illness. Now living alone in his small home, he got lonely most times. Jacob had one remaining relative, which was his sister Emilia.

She was one person that Jacob kept as number one on his mind, next to God of course. Emilia had become very ill and this worried Jacob. Jacob made a point to go visit his sister every day. He made her an Alubia pie each day. Alubia pie is made from a special sweet bean that only grows in Jacob's home town. Jacob enjoyed making Alubia pie for his sister to eat.

This day was not that different. Jacob woke up and said a prayer. He walked towards the front door to leave for the market. The market is where he went daily to get ingredients for the Alubia pie. However, on the way out the house Jacob heard a voice. The voice said "You will be tested three times, just do your best. Remember, if you pass these test, you will be in success." Jacob just thought that was strange, then he continued on his way.

When Jacob got to the market, the first person he saw was the grumpy store greeter. Jacob went by the store greeter smiling honestly at her. The greeter noticed him and responded. "Jacob why are you so darn happy every day?" Jacob answered! "Every day of life is truly a blessing, and we should always be grateful for what we have." Jacob went on his way and continued shopping. The grumpy store greeter looked towards Jacob with a new expression. She appeared to have understood exactly what he meant.

After purchasing the ingredients, Jacob went home to make the Alubia pie. Jacob gathered the finished pie, and started going towards his sister's house. He traveled through the dark forest, over the high hills, and between the deep valleys. On the way to his sister's house, he heard a constant pitter-patter around him. Was something following him? Jacob figured it must have just been the twigs and leaves falling. He continued walking to his sister's home.

When Jacob arrived at Emilia's house, he handed her the pie. He then noticed she was acting a little bit different. She had barely touched the pie for the visit. Jacob asked! "What is bothering you this morning Emilia?" She answered! "I am very worried. Jacob you are the only family I have, and you are always taking care of me.

I sometimes wonder who will take care of you when you truly need it." Jacob then became worried. Emilia felt bad and responded again. "Do you know what I'm even more upset about?" Jacob raised his eyes at her. She finished! "I'm worried about this yummy Alubia pie going to waste".

MAR
KET
ECM

Emilia then took a bite of her pie piece. Jacob's eyes glistened in relief while both laughed cheerfully. After Jacob returned home, he slept like a baby. The next day he woke up feeling well rested. Jacob got out of bed and said a prayer. Jacob then went out to the market, and purchased his usual ingredients for making Alubia pie. Strangely enough, the Store greeter was nowhere in sight on that day.

CHAPTER TWO
Caring for kittens

As Jacob stepped out of the market doors, he noticed a scared kitten on the curb. The kitten looked up at Jacob with such innocence. Right then, Jacob knew the kitten was lost. Jacob scooped the kitten up with one hand.

Jacob smiled at the kitten and said "I will raise you as if you were my own. No longer will you be alone." While leaving the market lot, Jacob was stopped once more. The store greeter rushed towards Jacob in a panic. She kept repeating "Jacob wait, wait up!" The kitten slightly jumped up as Jacob held her against his chest.

The greeter wailed as she caught up to him. "Jacob, I was reading the daily paper and came across an article, It mentioned the dark forest. You know, the one you cross every day. It says that strange things happen there. People have gone missing too. There's something scary waiting for lost townsmen who go into the woods. Please tell me you will stop going. You should not put yourself in danger." Jacob responded while still holding the kitten. "Thank you for letting me know this."

Jacob turned around and continued home. As soon as he got home, he gave a small bowl of milk to the kitten. Jacob cared for his sister so much, that even the greeters warning wouldn't stop him from visiting Emilia. Right then, Jacob realized it was time to visit Emilia.

Jacob slid the pie into a pie case. He just knew his sister was waiting for him. Jacob walked into the dark forest and felt like something evil was there. The thing seemed to follow him through the forest. At that point, Jacob became worried. Suddenly he heard a low sounding growl. Jacob then took off running. He ran past the forest, over the high hills, and towards the deep valley. On the way out of the high hills, Jacob stopped to catch his breath.

Just then, Jacob saw a hurt chic that had fallen from its tree nest. Jacob gently grasped the chick and returned it to the nest. When Jacob climbed down from the tree, he saw a bald eagle stare right at him. To Jacob, it almost seemed that the eagle was smiling at him. Jacob thought that was creepy. At that point Jacob started to wonder. 'How long was the eagle watching him, and did it really smile?' Jacob then continued on his journey towards Emilia's house.

COOK

CHAPTER THREE

Healing Emilia

Jacob continued through the deep valley. When Jacob reached Emilia's house, he was surprised to see how illuminated she was. Emilia was more active today than she had been in a long time. Emilia cooked plenty of food while waiting on Jacob's arrival.

Jacob looked at her face and saw how happy she seemed. Her whole face had a joyful glow. Maybe Emilia was not sick anymore? Emilia asked Jacob how his day was. Jacob started talking about the new kitten. Lastly, he told her about the creepy eagle predator.

Emilia laughed as she shouted "Eagles don't smile silly". Then she stopped and asked, "Why didn't you make a pie today?" Jacob played along while hiding the pie behind his back. Jacob answered! "All good things must come to an end right?" Emilia responded! "That's fine! I felt so good I made dessert, and supper for both of us today." She smiled at Jacob. Jacob was now shocked.

"Emilia you know I was only kidding right?" He then pulled the wrapped pie out of the small case. "Jacob you know I don't want you to leave anytime soon since I made all this food?" As the food continued to cook, Emilia pulled out a photo album. Her and Jacob reminisced about old times as the sun began to set. Jacob began to fill with happiness. He realized he would be spending the rest of the afternoon with his joy-filled sister.

When Jacob went home that night, he cuddled the kitten in his arms. After messaging the kitten's back, he placed it on the floor. As Jacob covered himself with the blanket, he saw the kitten jump back on the bed. Jacob tucked the kitten under the sheet and both fell asleep blissfully. Jacob woke the next morning feeling great, when suddenly he had an idea.

Instead of making another pie for his sister this morning, Jacob had another gift in mind. He had been thinking all morning about how much better Emilia had gotten from being sick. Wouldn't she feel better if she had the comfort, and warmth of a kitten? She seemed to have healed enough to care for a kitten.

Finally, Jacob decided he would give the kitten to Emilia. He started searching for the kitten. Hours and hours had passed, still no sign of the kitten. Jacob thought to himself that the poor kitten must have run away. Then, he finally gave up the search.

Soon the time came for Jacob to be on his way. Unfortunately, Jacob left with no gift this day. With no visit to see the store greeter, and no kitten, he started off today more lonely than ever before. Jacob was focused on giving Emilia all his attention. As Jacob began his daily journey, a rainstorm began. As usual, nothing stopped Jacob from showing his love to others. He sprinted through the dark forest with no interruptions. He rolled down the high hills excitedly. He jogged between the deep valleys with a smile on his face.

CHAPTER FOUR

Reward in keeping faith

When Jacob arrived at his sister's house, he saw an ambulance in front. Jacob was shocked and started to panic. Jacob ran to the first worker he saw and asked, "What is going on here?" The man answered as he laid one hand on Jacob's back. "Emilia has passed on, but there is something we have to give you. She told us to hold onto this envelope and give it to you when you came."

The worker apologized to Jacob, and wished him luck on his journey back. Jacob started crying! Everything the worker said went in one of Jacob's ears, and out the other. Jacob put the envelope in his pocket and turned back around.

Jacob slowly started dragging his feet towards the way back home. He was now making his way through the deep valley. Jacob kept crying while looking down at the muddy ground. Finally, Jacob reached a breaking point. Jacob fell down onto his knees. He sadly gazed into the mud as if it were his sanctuary. Jacob noticed the envelope had fallen and became covered in mud. He decided to open it to read what was inside.

Dear Jacob
Always Love Emilio

The letter wrote: "Dear Jacob, you are the only family I have left. I did not have many things at all. Otherwise, I would have saved them for you. No matter what, I had someone who loved me until my last day. Thank you Jacob! One thing I want you to do is know I am still happy. I am happy just like I was before my last day. Another thing I want you to do is be strong. Promise me you won't be saddened by my passing. Begin to find your true happiness in life. Stay strong because your blessing will come. Look forward at what life has to give you. Look up, and think ahead. With Love Always, Emilia!"

As Jacob continued to stare at the letter, He noticed how quiet the valley became. The thunderstorm had now passed. While Jacob was still on his knees, he repeated from the letter "Look up and think ahead". Jacob felt very uncertain. Suddenly he heard a voice call him. "Look up Jacob!"

Jacob stood up on his feet as he searched for that voice. "Jacob!" The voice called from the valley top. Jacob drew his eyes at the top of the valley and saw a figure. "I am karma! I have been sent especially for you, a giving soul. I was the market store greeter, the stranded kitten, and the fallen chick. You have shown that you are a person filled with good intentions, and you should be rewarded."

At first, Karma appeared as a beam of light on top of the valley. That light started moving from the top of the valley all the way to the ground. As the bottom of the light touched the valley ground, Jacob became speechless. Finally Karma began to change appearance.

First the bottom became feet, and then the entire light became human. Karma spoke! "Hello Jacob! I am in need of a friend because I am a lost giving soul myself. Could you help and guide me out of the deep valleys?" Watching Karma change appearance made Jacob realize he was sent an angel.

Since they were both giving souls, Jacob and Karma became closer over time. Jacob and Karma soon got married. They even raised their own children to become the best of kind hearts. Till this very day, it's said other angels still search those dark forest for lone townsmen with giving souls.

THE END

I am dedicating this book to my Son.